Grifyn

I feel like you don't get enough credit for your style.

GARBAGE DAY

P.

(handwritten, mirrored text):
Critique,
I feel like you don't
get enough credit for
your style.

◆ FriesenPress

One Printers Way
Altona, MB R0G 0B0
Canada

www.friesenpress.com

Copyright © 2024 by Domenic Pappas
First Edition — 2024

Cover illustration by Nicholas Donovan Mueller

ISBN
978-1-03-919632-2 (Hardcover)
978-1-03-919631-5 (Paperback)
978-1-03-919633-9 (eBook)

1. FICTION, NATURE & THE ENVIRONMENT

Distributed to the trade by The Ingram Book Company

PREFACE

Before you embark on the extraordinary journey that contains the intrusive thoughts in my mind, I would like to tell all readers this scripture is a culmination of what ifs. What if Santa Claus was real? What if you took that bold step and sent a corporate message to Gwen in accounting calling out her passive-aggressive emails? I believe holding the mindset of 'what if' keeps us youthful. It is a crucial factor when coming up with a story. Questioning your surroundings and applying your perspective to any given situation allows each of us to showcase our unique individualism. This story is a chain link reaction of what if's, shaped by the tapestry of the experiences of my life.

ACKNOWLEDGEMENTS

I would like to thank all the garbage workers for their service, doing the dirty jobs — in rain, sleet, and snow — that keep our communities clean. I would also like to thank Cory Lupovici (AKA Cory Poopoopeepee) for helping me with the direction of this story. To Adonis, my partner's father, who believes in my imagination and was instrumental in convincing Marina that their daughter should not break up with me. When we first met, I had sold myself short. I do not know why my opening line when introducing myself was that I failed Spanish in grade ten. Hopefully now you can see my vision and that I am a man with ambition who is more than just somebody with a below average understanding of the Spanish language. Shoutout to the homies Miguel and Jaren for originally brainstorming this idea with me. Our group chat has been an incubator for many insane ideas and they all bring me great joy.

GARBAGE DAY

DOMENIC PAPPAS

CHAPTER

Whoosh! Reggie, listening to surfer rock through headphones, pretends he's in an ocean barrel gliding through the Pacific. In reality, he's riding the tailgate of a garbage truck at forty kilometres an hour with Chuck driving up front. Still, though, it's a premium rush. He feels like an urban Kelly Slater, especially in the intense, hot summer months. Everything smells worse in the heat, and shade is nowhere to be found. Despite this, Chuck and Reggie valiantly ride their iron steed full of trash through the sun, shirts off, and acquire golden, god-like tans. Women approach them on their days off, thinking they're lifeguards. Children are always fascinated by the truck itself, cheering and waving at them from the back seat of their car as they drive by. Occasionally, kids will get tours of the garbage truck, getting to see all the controls and the cockpit. It's like a fire truck tour on a budget. For the kids whose parents entertain them with a garbage truck tour, it's an experience they never forget. For the parents of said kids, "it's just a phase" is their hope. But today, a lucky group of students is about to get the ultimate tour.

As Chuck is waiting for Reggie to collect some bins, a few kids walking to school looked up to him in awe.

"Hey! You guys wanna see somethin' cool?" Chuck shouts through his window, looking down at the schoolkids.

Reggie, throwing some trash in the back of the loader, then warns everyone to stand back. He then picks one kid out of the group and tells him, "Hit that lever and run like hell!"

The overjoyed student pulls back what he would call a joystick and runs to safety as if he had just sparked the wick of his first cherry bomb. He and his mates watch the machine slowly rise, waiting for the carnage to unfold. As the claw pierces bags of garbage, it hits an old jug of milk. Everyone in the splash zone gets lit up like they're courtside at SeaWorld, but instead of cold, crisp water, it was more like Shamu's spoiled lunch. Reggie and Chuck are unphased and carry on with their route.

"Stay in school, kids!" Reggie yells from the back of the truck as it speeds away. The kids can't stop laughing at the awesomeness of the explosion.

"Faaam! That was bussin!" one of the kids exclaims.

"Deadass though, mans went in!" says another. They can't wait to go to school and show off their sour clothes.

On especially hot days, certain houses leave cold refreshments on the steps for the garbage workers. People are extremely caring at times. Every once in a while, this one house leaves out a six-pack of glass Pepsi bottles so cold they are almost frozen, as is the case today. Chuck and Reggie take a minute to rest after they chug them — nothing is more refreshing than an ice-cold pop after hours of manual labour in thirty-degree weather — not too long of a break, however. Once their route is done, they get to go home. Whether it takes four hours or a whole day, the pay remains the same. So they usually maintain a quick pace. Safety isn't always the number one factor. After a co-worker got hit by a car, the reflective vests became mandatory. Every day, they have to dodge vehicles angrily overtaking the truck, whether it's due to road rage, being late for work, or having an urgent sense of needing to poo. The workers have to remain cognizant of their surroundings or they'll be flattened by a Nissan Sentra.

As far as morning traffic goes, today is the culmination of the worst of the worst: shut down highways, accidents, construction, the works. And as all morning commutes are during the rush of the hour, this one sustains much friction. Making his way through the litter of taxis, transit, unqualified Uber's, scooters, and cyclists, the only thing keeping Bernie from losing his sanity and going ten-pin bowling down the sidewalk with his Acura is the promise of a steamy cup of java. Bernie has a special bond with his coffee. More than an energizing beverage, his coffee is a warm friend, not only to his hands but to his body and soul. Even a granule of sugar too much in his two milk, half sugar dark roast is enough to ruin his entire day. So you can imagine the instant feeling of irritation he feels when the street leading to his caffeinated haven has been closed for no apparent reason. *That's no problem. I'll take the next street*, he thinks to himself. Unbeknownst to Bernie, today is only filled with losing battles. Off to the next street he goes. Upon hastily rounding the corner, there is a halt accompanied by car horns and sporadic hand signals. Having already committed to the turn, Bernie is now stationery, boxed in by the traffic ahead and behind. It only takes a few moments for him to exit the vehicle and see what the root of this commotion is.

As Bernie approaches the crux of chaos on Pendrell Street, he notices a large garbage truck trying to turn down a narrow alley.

"I'll guide you through!" he yells over the sound of an industrial diesel engine as it idles with a rough knocking sound. The garbage man, whose vest is stitched with the name 'Chuck', points at the driveway opening while mouthing something. Bernie walks towards the cockpit as the window rolls down.

"The car is parked too close to the driveway! Reverse your car back onto the main road, and I'll go around to the next block," says Chuck.

Bernie answers back civilly. "There's no need for

all of these cars to reverse. I'll guide you through. You have enough space."

Chuck gives Bernie the same response. "That vehicle isn't six feet from the driveway!"

Bernie must now repeat himself as well. "I can see how much space there is. You'll be okay. Just turn the wheel all the way before you start to move!"

Once again, Chuck responds, "That vehicle isn't parked six feet from the driveway!"

This argument is a closed loop. Each time gets more and more irritating to the other party until Bernie's fuse burns out. With no coffee to comfort his soul, Bernie reaches a breaking point.

"Just move the truck out of the way, you stupid fuck!"

The garbage truck emits a high-pitched and quick release of pressure as the air brakes engage. Chuck then opens his door and climbs down the steps. A tall, skinny, spikey-haired, squirrely-eyed Chuck is now walking towards Bernie, towering over him as his steel-toe boots give him a few extra inches of height and a few extra kilograms of stability.

"You think you can yell at me, little man? Huh?"

Tension down the block has built and people are now hopelessly getting out of their vehicles, accepting that they will be stuck there for a while longer. The commotion between Bernie and Chuck has surpassed verbal. The pressure cooker is about to burst. Both parties are getting physical. The mixed crowd of commuters are now all out of their vehicles, picking sides to cheer for, creating a divide. Many of them are filming on their phones, chanting for violence, hoping to get a viral-worthy video.

"WORLDSTAR!" Yells one scruffy nomad moseying along drunkenly. Bernie stares deeply into the eyes of Chuck. Chuck stares intensely back. Don't get passionate eye contact confused for romance. This is far from love at first sight—more along the lines of all's fair in love and war. Chuck recognizes this and weakly attempts to diffuse the emotional moment.

"Get back in your car buddy. We don't want the paramedics to scrape you off the street."

"You're not that guy, pal. You're not that guy," says Bernie as his eyes widen, getting into Chuck's face.

"Oh yeah?" says Chuck confidently.

"Trust me, pal. You're not that guy," Bernie restates, softly pushing Chuck backward with his big belly. Upon a sudden movement, the crowd erupts with deafening enthusiasm.

CHAPTER

Sharp introductory music plays for the start of Channel Eight news. Clarity and warmth from the news anchors' voices greet the viewers.

"Hello everybody. I'm Pinky Mayes."

"And I'mmm Michael Disco! Today's top story: Carpet stain!" the male anchor says as the production crew waves to him, mouthing his mistake. Michael corrects himself. "What? Garbage stain? Sorry about that everybody. Autocorrect, am I right? Today's top story: Garbage day!"

Co-anchor Pinky describes further. "Here is a look at the scene today between a garbage truck driver and a local commuter." The video begins with Pinky's narration as follows. "This altercation broke out as a garbage truck blocked both flows of traffic earlier today. Some scenes are quite graphic so viewer discretion is advised. What seems like an obvious disagreement quickly turns into a chaotic brawl. People start getting out of their cars and applauding as the situation becomes more aggressive. You can see other commuters burning their trash and throwing it into the ring where the two individuals are fighting. The crowd continues cheering on the violence and even looting the nearby convenience store as smoke from the fire clouds the area. Meanwhile, the garbage truck driver and local commuter carry on battling as each assailant bleeds profusely while grappling the collar of the other, pulling and tearing their clothes during the process. After a rampage of punches and elbows, you hear a warning howled as looters barrel their way out of the convenience store: 'COPS!' That's when all the commuters involved split in different directions like a high school house party that just got raided by police."

Michael shifts the attention to the reaction online this video has caused. "Currently trending number three online, here is what the Twitterverse is saying."

@BoatsNbros says "F*** garbage trucks! They are loud, obnoxious, and slow like my girl-friend's British bulldog. What are people even throwing out anyways??? #CompostNation"

@DropCliffsNotBombs says "The unfortunate product cycle of cheap consumer goods. Pollution caused by unregulated manufactur-ing. Shipped overseas with tankers carrying illegal substances polluting our waters. Finally sold to a Western throwaway culture that has been taught to produce waste for convenience. #triggered"

@DieselDaddy says "They are doing the dirty jobs that no one else wants to do! How would you feel having people yell at you all day for picking up their trash? #KnowYourPrivilege"

@EnvironmentalMama says "The idea of garbage cleanup in theory should be obsolete. Compostable packaging or package-free busi-nesses like @BYOP allow you to get supplies without wasting precious resources. Or buy local. Help the community and get something that will last a lifetime. #love"

Pinky offers her opinion on the tweets shown. "Those are some good points. It seems global warming is here to stay, and the heatwave this year nearly killed me. I think I'll start doing my part to achieve zero waste. What do you say, Michael? One week from now, let's bring all the non-compostable waste we've generated on air and see who has less?"

"You're on, Pinky! Loser gets the winner's garbage dumped on them!" Both laughing nervously, they accept the challenge.

"Okay, viewers, let us know who you think will win using the hashtag 'DumpOff,' and feel free to challenge your friends and family with the hashtag yourselves." Both anchors laugh as the network transitions to its next story. Michael looks over at the camera to his left as his face transitions to a more serious demeanour.

"In other news today, can cats read?"

As the story continues, Eugenio Violante takes specific notice of this headline. He is the owner of the garbage enterprise in question by the media just now, Wastefellas Garbage Co. Nobody knows if his last name was birthed by lineage or in the streets due to his history of violent crimes. Regardless, being head of the sanitation enterprise brings responsibility for another organization. La Cosa Nostra, the mob, or as most people around town refer to it, the Mafia.

Mr. Violante and his soldiers are discussing how to handle this bad press. One of their immediate reactions is traditional in this line of business. "Hey boss, you want me to take care of this guy?"

Eugenio shoots that idea down. He logs into the company computer and looks up the employee records, ascertaining the names of the two employees who worked that route today. As far as mom-and-pop operations go, this is far from it. The business is run without much supervision, so it's not a surprise something like this has happened.

Waiting for Eugenio's orders, Franky goes to the fridge and pulls out sandwich materials. "You guys gotta try this prosciutto." Franky rips off a piece and stuffs it in his mouth.

"Oof, that'll shine the sun over Santa Maria's Basilica on a cloudy day." Jimmy grabs a piece of focaccia and indulges himself. "Lorenzo, you gotta try this," says Jimmy in awe of the flavour.

"Nah, I can't. I'm intermittent fasting," says Lorenzo respectfully.

"What the hell is an intermittent fasting? I never heard of nothin' like that before in my life," says a confused Franky.

"It's good for the digestion. Plus, they use all those nitrates in the meats now. They'll kill you."

Franky gets irritated and somewhat offended at Lorenzo's attempt to be healthier. "Uhhh, earth to braciole. My Nonno dry aged this in his basement for nine months with nothin' but salt."

Lorenzo lightens up and responds. "If it's from Mario's basement then I gotta have some. Gimme a couple slices for tomorrow. I have a gluten-free loaf that would pair with it beautifully for breakfast."

"It would be a fuckin' crime to put that pro-sciutto on some gluten-free bullshit. What's a matter for you lately, Lorenzo? I find some risotto in this guy's fridge the other day and take a bite. Fuckin' cauliflower rice. The disrespect," says Jimmy, clutch-ing his thumb and forefinger together.

Lorenzo laughs. "It's good for ya, what do you want me to say? You gotta take care a yaself."

Franky throws in his two cents on the topic. "You know, that's what's wrong with society today. No grit. We got gluten-free mobsters and meatless meatballs. You know what meatballs are without meat? They're just balls. The whole world is snackin' on cojones."

Eugenio finally opens a file matching one of the employees who was on the route in question:

14

Chuck McBinny.

"This is not good. This is not good. Bring Chuck to me. I need to talk to him," Says Eugenio, preparing a sandwich.

"Sure thing, boss," Jimmy replies. After butting his cigarette out in an exquisite crystal glass ashtray, he rounds up Lorenzo and Franky to start a manhunt for Chuck. Eugenio turns the TV back on and is too focused on the next news story to notice his soldiers leaving. He watches cats read while he draws smoke from a slow-burning Cuban whose cherry combusts into a crumble. White ash floats down onto his thick gold necklace intertwined with his grey chest hair.

The soldiers pile into Jimmy's car. An absolutely breathtaking willow green 1973 Buick Riviera. Naturally, when you stuff a bunch of mobsters into an American classic that isn't a Cadillac, there's going to be an argument.

"You know I love this car, Jimmy, I really do. But nothin' drives like a Cadillac," says Lorenzo from the back while laying on a bench of plush cream leather.

"Your caddy drives like a drunken sailor!" says Jimmy, driving with a grin on his face.

"I got a race engine! Whaddaya got?!" replies a comfortable Lorenzo.

"Take it easy. I'll give it to you, Cadillacs are nice. But you can't beat a Buick Riviera, you just can't. I don't know what to tell you! It's scientifically impossibl—"

"Alright, alright, pull over here. It's the house on the corner," Franky intervenes from the passenger seat, stabilizing the situation. Jimmy pulls tight to the curb while mumbling under his breath, knowing the argument is going nowhere.

Inside the house, Chuck's wife Patty is preparing an extravagant cake for their son's nineteenth birthday. This is their last year with Horace before he heads off for college. It's somewhat close to home, only a few hours' drive. However, Chuck and his wife are experiencing pre-empty nest syndrome and want to make his last birthday with them special. As Patty scrapes some batter into the garburator, Chuck shouts from the couch in the living room.

"You're gonna clog the pipes! Throw it in the compost!"

She responds stubbornly. "It's fine. It's what the garburator is for!"

"Listen, honey, perishables are for the compost. Papers and plastics are for recycling. Everything else goes in the trash to the landfill. It's a system! I can't have people knowing our trash isn't sorted properly. It's just bad for business!"

DING DONG! The doorbell rings, and Chuck is once again distracted from watching the daily news. He gets up in an irritated fashion and opens the front door to be greeted by three sharply dressed Italians.

"You Chuck?" Franky asks. Chuck has a pretty good idea of who's asking, but inquires anyway.

"Yeah, who's askin'?" he says sternly.

Jimmy gets impatient. "Get in the car. Boss wants to talk to ya. We'll have you home before that delicious-smelling cake cools down on your pretty little windowsill."

Chuck shouts to his wife. "Honey, Eugenio wants to see me. I'll be right back!" He puts on a jacket and responds to Jimmy as he closes the front door. "Pies are for windowsills, not cakes."

Jimmy looks back at Chuck with bombastic side eye as they walk towards the car. "Eh?" he questions.

"You said you'll have me home before that cake cools down on my windowsill. That's not the saying. You don't cool *cakes* on windowsills. You cool *pies* on windowsills."

Jimmy looks back irritatedly and responds, "Don't be a schmuck, Goldilocks. This isn't a fairy tale. Get in the car." He lights up another cigarette.

"You know the fairy tale, but you don't know the dessert?" Chuck says, questioning Jimmy further.

"You give the boss some smart-ass lip like that tonight and he'll cauterize your ass shut with the cherry of his cigar," Franky chimes in. "I've seen him do it. Couldn't eat seared tuna for a month. I'd prefer not to see him do it again." He opens the door, directing Chuck into the back.

"How often do you eat seared tuna? Wait a second — woah. Is that a seventy-three Buick?" Chuck says in envy.

Jimmy humbly responds, "That's mine." They pile in and Jimmy cranks the ignition. The rumble of a Detroit V8 engine floods the cabin with sound and vibration as they head back to Eugenio.

"Wow, it's a beautiful ride man," Chuck remarks in awe.

"Yeah, thanks kid." That compliment is the only thing keeping Jimmy from telling Chuck to shut his chippy little mouth.

After Chuck basks in the nostalgia and a few moments of peace and quiet pass, he says out loud to everyone, "But *nothin'* beats a Cadillac."

Lorenzo and Franky cackle. Jimmy turns up the radio and takes another drag from his tobacco stick to the orchestral sounds of Ennio Morricone.

Back at the news studio, the nightly broadcast is over. Michael Disco applauds the crew and heads to his dressing room. He has a ritual after every broadcast. What he refers to as a ritual, others might certainly refer to as an addiction. Being sharp for one hour straight on live television is stressful. So after every broadcast, he likes to blow off steam. Once he gets to his dressing room, Michael sits in front of the mirror and starts to make up news stories.

"Tonight on the eight o' clock news: time traveller appears, urging a halt to gender reveal parties. But now, is there a *twenty-seventh* letter? We go live to Steve's Bait & Tackle Shop to find out." Michael's head dips down under the mirror as he snorts aggressively. Popping back up quickly, his face is covered in white powder. Eyes wide open, he exclaims, "Newsflash! I love cocaine!"

Michael gets up to open the door after hearing three subtle knocks. The party girls he scheduled have arrived. Upon entry they are greeted by three things: Michael Disco, cocaine, and a speaker booming Benny Benassi. Michael starts to dance foolishly with his new entertainment, throwing dollar bills as they bump and grind on him.

"It doesn't get any better than being a local news anchor!" Michael yells out to himself. The girls woo in affirmation.

"Yeah, Michael! Report this!" says one dancer, ripping open her shirt as she flashes Michael. He submerges his head into an anthill of cocaine and continues raving.

Outside his dressing room are two large security guards dressed in all black making sure nobody interrupts his ritual. Pinky hears a constant thumping bass drum.

♪ BOOM! BOOM! BOOM! BOOM! BOOM! BOOM! BOOM! BOOM! ♪

She approaches the door defenders and asks to get in. The bouncers look at their clipboard. Turning over the pages, they cannot find her name.

"Sorry, Pinky. Michael didn't add you to the guestlist. Great job tonight though! I'll tell Michael you came through. Maybe we can get you on the list for tomorrow." Pinky expresses her gratitude and heads home. The bass continues as she exits the lobby.

♪ *BOOM! BOOM! BOOM! BOOM! BOOM! BOOM! BOOM! BOOM!* ♪

CHAPTER

The next day is quickly showcasing changes in public behaviour in response to the previous day's news story. Bernie and his wife approach the outdoor shopping plaza where a zero-waste packaging store, BYOP, is located. The masses seem to have beaten them there. Cars are crammed in every available spot, including the sidewalks and street. Lineups of people wrap around the centre of the square. Bernie is shocked by the number of people he sees advocating for environmentalism. The lineup is too long for any average person to wait for groceries, but it seems as though a lot of people are waiting just to be a part of something, a part of the movement. Bernie and his wife join the lineup partially for this reason. They always enjoy watching mass chaos together. They see Black Friday at Walmart not as an opportunity to save money on home goods, but as a form of entertainment. Mostly, they join because neither of them want to go to another grocery store where they would accumulate packaging waste, lose the #DumpOff, and be showered with garbage.

Across the street is a related but separate movement: sanitation workers protesting the character and view of their industry in the mainstream lens. Many of the garbage workers held picketing signs with messages such as:

More pay, less garbage!

We take out your crap, and you give us shit?

Garbage lives matter.

Garbage CAN. Not garbage CAN'T!

With the lineup at BYOP extending down the street, there is some crossfire between the two parties. People are reacting to the signs held up by sanitation workers.

"Oh boo hoo! You want more pay to collect the garbage? Go back to college and get a better job then!" whoops out Gary, a local waiting in line across from the protest.

"Fuck you, Gary! I know you don't recycle your batteries!" fires back Reggie, recognizing him.

"Hey! You can't look through my trash! Didn't you take an oath or something?" Gary screams back across the road.

"Yeah, I took an oath that says you can lick my balls!" The sanitation workers laugh in unison and high-five each other. Gary mumbles under his breath and moves around the corner as the line gets shorter.

With so much attention on this corner, it's inevitable a news crew will show up to find out what the deeper story is. Right on time, the Channel Eight news crew squeaks their way into the parking lot in an old white van.

"Over there! That's the shot!" field reporter Nigel Dansby says to his crew urgently. Stationed in between the divide of the sanitation protest and the newly inspired environmentalists, the film crew sets up as quickly as they can. Soon enough they are rolling, with the left side of the frame showing environmentalists and the right side of the frame showing sanitation protests. Nigel is smack in the middle of the great divide as he starts to report.

"Behind me to my right are the frontlines of an eco-friendly frenzy. Across this no man's land to my left, we have the sanitation workers demanding respect." Nigel walks over to the lineup at BYOP, asking a young couple waiting in line why they are here.

"I like coming here because after I fill my container, I can snack a little while walking around. It's like getting samples at Costco but more exciting," the overjoyed boyfriend responds while getting a friendly slap on the shoulder from his girlfriend.

"You're so bad! It's nice that more people are starting to understand their impact. That said, I also like to sneak in a couple chocolate-covered pretzels while I'm cruising the aisles. Saving the environment one snac—"

Nigel clutches his finger to his ear, interrupting her. "We've just received word that Gigi has pulled up to the protest! We're heading over now to get an exclusive look!"

Gigi is the hottest thing in activism at the moment. Her protest on mute dolphins has just gone global. Madonna, Zendaya, Kobe, Bono, Beyoncé, and now added to that list of names, Gigi—pop culture celebrities with elitist status that means they only need one name to be recognized. Originally, years ago, Gigi got the media's attention for her protest in Europe, exposing a slaughterhouse and referring to their employees as 'so not woke.' Since then, every protest she's attended has gone viral.

Every issue she touches on turns to gold. Having her at this protest is massive for the town because, lucky for them, Gigi's number one priority right now is climate change. So after Nigel exclaims her arrival, he rushes over to an electric limo surrounded by paparazzi and fans. The bodyguard comes out to open the curbside door, then Gigi's legs emerge. The electronic drum and bass music of Ke$ha floods the ears of everyone nearby as the windows vibrate to a deep resonance. Flashes start to strobe as she struts out of the limo and towards the lineup at BYOP.

"Gigi, over here! Gigi! GIGI!" yell the paparazzi, trying to get a photo. Her fans are screaming, holding out photos to get an autograph. Surrounded by flashing lights and screaming fans, Gigi signs as many posters as she can before the crowd gets too rowdy. Her bodyguard clears a path to exit the commotion. They escort her to a stage with a platform and microphone set up. She stands confidently at the mahogany podium and adjusts the microphone to her mouth. Gigi looks over to her bodyguard for reassurance.

"You got this," he mouths compassionately while nodding his head to Gigi. She takes a deep breath and begins her speech.

"Climate change is bad. Like really bad. Climate change is really, really, really bad." The crowd goes wild. "If you wanna throw something in the garbage, just like, don't."

Within minutes, the speech has been retweeted by the likes of several celebrities including Oprah, Michelle Obama, and Kourtney Kardashian. Among the exhilaration, a battle for a parking spot in the tightly compacted lot is going down.

CRASH! Two cars collide and both drivers get out shouting madly at one another. Everyone in the crowd turns around in unison upon the impact, except for one person who is completely infatuated with Gigi. Moments ago, all eyes were on her, but now she can only see one face in the crowd. In the middle of a sea of hairy heads facing the opposite way, Gigi locks eyes with Horace. She is staring passionately back, mostly because of the residual adrenaline from that powerful speech, but not completely. As the crowd begins to face back toward Gigi, Horace's presence begins to blur among the horde, eventually disappearing completely.

"My goodness! She is incredible!" exclaims Nigel as he continues with the story. He walks across the street with the intent of ascertaining the sanitation workers' frustration. They are eager to express themselves on camera, and Nigel can feel the tension as he approaches them while they scream to the public.

"We are not going to accept this ongoing disrespect from the public!" Support from the surrounding sanitation workers is shown by cheering after every point.

Chuck steps forward. "Yeah! These wannabe environmentalists kill me. You wouldn't believe the things we find in their garbage! They say we're dirty workers, but their garbage tells a different tale."

Nigel dives deeper into that point while garbage men chant around the camera. "What are some of the most surprising items you've found while sorting through the trash here?"

Reggie interrupts and pulls the microphone to his mouth. "Two weeks ago, I found an entire garbage bag filled with batteries and magnets. All AA batteries. Who uses that many batteries? Not to mention those are supposed to be recycled! Motha fuckas be up to some shit, Nigel. Magnetic fields and shit."

Nigel faces the camera and puts in his conclusion on the debate. "Well, there you have it. You heard it here, folks. Mother effers be up to some shiznit. Looks like everyone has something to hide.

Sanitation workers are the secret holders in the shadows, and the light is now shining brightly upon them. Michael, back to you at the studio."

"Very powerful stuff, Nigel. I can only hope they get to the bottom of their magnetic field dilemma. Now, we have Eugenio Violante, CEO of Wastefellas Garbage Co, live via video call with us." As the screen splits down the middle, Eugenio appears, ready to address the public. "Welcome on. Long time no see, Mr. Violante. First question. What's going on in the garbage business?"

"I'll tell you what's goin' on. My guys are gettin' harassed day in day out. I want to use this time to ask the public to show a little respect," says Eugenio, setting the tone.

"You know, you guys over at the news station don't make my life very friggin' peaceful. Makin' my business look like a problem. We're doin' the public a service. What do we get for it? Hostility."

Michael butts in to defend the media. "We simply bring light to what is going on in the community. You don't want to be in the news, don't have any public outbursts."

"Woulda been nice to get a phone call about our side of the story before airing this bullsh—"

Michael interrupts Eugenio, knowing what

word he was about to say. "This is a live broadcast, Mr. Violante."

Eugenio continues on with some positive changes in the making. "Anyways. We've been communicating with the farmers in the area. We'll be milling compost at our facility and sending it to local farms free of charge. They're concerned about the increasing price of fertilizer. This will save them money and reduce precious real estate in the landfill." Eugenio pauses for a moment and takes a smooth drag of his cigar.

"A win-win for everybody! Any other changes, Mr. Violante?"

Eugenio responds after calmy blowing a thick cloud of smoke into the camera lens. "Yes, this one will take some time, but it will be revolutionary. We've collaborated with an autonomous transport company to have emission-free, remotely operated electric collection vehicles. The only thing we ask from the public is to replace their waste bins with our newly designed garbage cans to facilitate efficient collection."

Mr. Disco is pleasantly surprised at the efforts Eugenio has made to combat the problem. "How much are families expected to pay for a new set of these garbage bins?" Mr. Disco starts a condescending tone.

"We're still testing materials. Might be around fifty bucks for a set. Maybe as high as a hundred bucks," says Eugenio, nodding his head.

"With about fifty thousand homes in the area, at a hundred bucks a pop, I guess my five-million-dollar question is this: Will this truly help our community, or is this an opportunity to line your pockets?" Mr. Disco says with a stern look on his face.

Eugenio, caught off guard, responds as politely as possible, even though he can feel his head steaming at these accusations. "What we are doing is for the public. It has been demanded by the public. Why don't we break into your books? Where's your money goin'?"

Michael responds condescendingly. "If I don't ask, somebody else will. Typically, if there's a story to be found, you gotta follow the money. The money never lies." Michael throws his hands up in the air.

"I'm in the business of waste management. And in my line of work, you follow the trash, not the money. There's no glamour in it, but my employees put focaccia on the table. If I wanted to be an overpraised yabbo, I woulda tried to be a news anchor."

Michael laughs nervously as he closes out the interview. "The news gives our community critical information, Mr. Violante. I take pride in delivering it to the people every night. We look forward to seeing these new advances lead the environmental charge." Mr. Disco smiles at the camera, waiting for Eugenio's final statement.

"Critical information?" Eugenio says, questioning Michael's integrity.

"That's right, Mr. Violante. Critical information," responds a prideful Michael.

"I watched you babble on for seven minutes about whether or not cats can read. One thing you don't realize about critical information, Mr. Disco, is that *garbage* is information."

A confused Michael stares into the camera for a few moments of dead air as Eugenio smirks with a cigar in his mouth. "Yes, well that's all the time we have unfortunately. Good luck with your development, and I'm sure we'll have you back on once it's completed."

The news pans back to full screen as Eugenio's video disconnects. Co-anchor Pinky Mayes sprinkles in a comment before the next story is headlined. "Great interview, Michael! I'm proud of the stand you took. What we do here is important, and Mr.

Violante's belittling undertone towards your integrity was just rude."

"Thank you, Pinky. There's no one I'd rather do this with every night." Michael and Pinky smile and face the camera as she introduces the next story with pure confidence.

"In other news. Do fish really *need* water? Studies may suggest otherwise."

Eugenio, watching the story from his office, turns off his television and decides to check in on the development of the new collection vehicles. He hops in his villainous, black Maserati Quattroporte and sets course to the lab. Upon entering the workshop, Eugenio is greeted by a symphony of loud buzzing and drilling. The maestro of this madness, the lead engineer, looks over and immediately recognizes Eugenio. He welcomes him in and offers a firm handshake in excitement, eager to show the progress he has made with his new technology.

"Mr. Violante! You may not remember me, but I'm Torgen. You put me in charge of this revolutionary project some weeks ago. They are running some tests out back right now. Come take a look!" Torgen scans his employee card to access the back room and holds the door for Eugenio. Eugenio stands in the doorway, speechless. Torgen then waves him through while beginning to explain the progress he has made.

"Its action is very simple. Once the vehicle approaches the garbage bin, a clamp squeezes the top, popping off the lid, while another arm lifts the bin upside down into the bed of the collector. The waste is then compressed to maximise its capacity." He rearranges his spectacles, eagerly awaiting Eugenio's response.

"Can I try using it?" Eugenio curiously asks.

Torgen replies worriedly. "It is very untraditional for clients to participate in the testing stages." Eugenio remains unresponsive with a stern mug. "But ... I don't see how anything could go wrong," says Torgen, intimidated.

Eugenio smiles and takes a seat near a large controller with the labels *lift*, *direction*, *compress*, *right arm*, and *left arm* on the casing. Torgen points at the controls and slowly explains.

"So all you need to do is point the direction knob towards the bin, then when you are near it, engage the arms to lift the bin."

Eugenio does exactly what Torgen says and is amazed as the garbage bin gets lifted off the ground. "Can this thing deliver pizzas too?" Eugenio says with a grin on his face.

"It can do whatever you pay us to make it do!" Torgen corporately says. They both laugh as Torgen instructs Eugenio on how to place the garbage bin back down. "All that's left to do is disengage the arms and compress the load." Torgen points to the *compress* button and nods. The punchy sounds of everything snapping, crackling, popping, and being crushed take over as the compressor in the collection vehicle ungracefully reduces the load to less than half of its original size.

CRUNCH! BANG! CHOMP! POP!

Eugenio's eyes light up while witnessing its barbaric, mechanical power. "Is this thing ready to hit the streets, Torgen?"

"We still have to run some diagnostics and refine the software, but it should be ready in a week or so," Torgen says, to the relief of Eugenio.

"Once we get a fleet of these running, I can get everyone off my back and return to business as usual. Thanks, Torgen. Talk to you soon." Eugenio heads back to his car, breathing a heavy sigh of relief.

CHAPTER

Gigi and Horace have been texting for a few days after exchanging numbers at the protest. Finally, they've decided to go on a date. The two young adults awkwardly sit at the park, having a picnic on a beautiful day and pulling up TikTok on their phones as they laugh at the trending #DumpOff videos.

"Have you seen this one?" says Horace giddily. He proceeds to show her a video from @DieselDaddy with one sorry loser getting the entire bed of a dump truck filled with garbage poured over the top of him. As their laughter tapers, Gigi asks Horace about his passion for the environment. He hesitates for a moment. Horace hears from Chuck every day about how wasteful so many people are, about the interesting and weird things Chuck finds scattered around the landfill. So Horace fears if he tells Gigi what his father does for a living, she will think less of him. Gigi is so passionate about climate change, he doesn't want to start the date on a sour note. So instead, he tells her a different, but true, story: the story of Chuck's past.

Eugenio Violante didn't grow up in a family with the status or financial well-being that he had accrued as an adult. After high school, he applied to be a labourer for Wastefellas Garbage Co. It was good money right away, and he didn't know if schooling was right for him—not that he or his parents could afford it. As a garbageman, you always come across interesting items in people's trash. In Eugenio's case, it was a baby. One day, Eugenio popped the lid off a metal bin, and laying on a clumpy bag of trash was an infant. It was crying and kicking. Eugenio had no idea what to do so he brought it up front and strapped the baby boy to the passenger seat. When they brought the truck back to HQ after their route, Eugenio took the baby to the boss. They discussed taking it to an orphanage, but the boss didn't like the idea of sending it off like that.

"I guess we gotta name it then?" Eugenio said, looking to his boss, Aldo for ideas.

"Where was the dumpster you found him in?" said Aldo, looking at his desk.

"The one in the alley just past Baltimore Avenue," Eugenio said as he waved his arms to the East.

"Well, somebody chucked him in a dumpster. How about Chuck?" Aldo confirmed confidently.

"Hey ya know what? He kinda looks like a Chuck. I like it. What do you think, little guy?"

Eugenio looked down at young Chuck playing with his arms like he was raving at an after-hours club freely. The baby shrieked and laughed.

"Eugenio, can you dig an old crib out of the landfill, maybe some toys too? Clean 'em up and put them in the break room. He'll have plenty of company throughout the day. I'll get the janitors to feed him and change his diapers between shifts. Put his crib in a dark meeting room at night so he can sleep." Eugenio, holding the baby, got up and went to fix Chuck up with his new room and board. He's about to close the door and looks back.

"What about his last name, boss? Ya know, in case of like, legal stuff." Eugenio inquiries casually.

"Eh, just give 'em my last name. McBinny, Chuck McBinny. Nobody will question a McBinny." Aldo says assuredly. Eugenio smiles and leaves Aldo to his work.

The guys grew to like having him around, especially Eugenio. He always took a few minutes out of his day to play with the little guy or read him a story. Wastefellas was a twenty-four-hour operation, so he was always under someone's watchful eye. All of the baby's milestones happened at the landfill, from his first steps to his first words and everything in between. The guys in the breakroom all had bets on what the baby's first word would be. 'Dada' was the heavy favourite. But everyone went crazy when the day finally came.

"Trash!" the baby exclaimed one day. It wasn't surprising considering his surroundings at the time. Money was finally exchanged for the lucky winners of the bet.

"This kid is my good luck charm! Hey, who do ya got on the Celtics game tonight?" one of the guys said, laughing obnoxiously.

As time went on, the baby grew into a boy. Everyone pitched in to set him up with the essentials for his first day of kindergarten: juice boxes, crayons, and a brand new pair of light-up Sketchers. He would ride on the back of the garbage truck to school every morning with whatever crew was working the route near the elementary school. Hopping off the back of a truck with a bunch of tough-looking guys while his shoes were flashing like a lighthouse was a statement noticed by the other seven-year-olds. When the crew had finished their route, they would swing by the school on their way back to the landfill and pick him up. It was the perfect system.

They say it takes a village to raise a child. In this case, it took a landfill. Regardless, Chuck was always looked after well. As the years went on, Chuck entered high school. Through his pubescence, he always turned heads from the girls. He looked like such a badass hopping off that truck every morning. They were attracted to his mysterious spirit. Being associated with a crew of muscular, tanned dudes wasn't a bad thing either. His social life thrived as a teenager without a whole lot of supervision. He never had a curfew. If he wanted to go home all he needed to do was find a garbage truck and hitch a ride. Eugenio would check in now and then, making sure his grades were alright. Chuck was a steady C+ student with the occasional B in physical education. That was good enough to keep Eugenio from cracking down on him. But like any teenager, he got into his fair dose of trouble: kicking in fences, putting fireworks in mailboxes, throwing paintballs into traffic, and even smoking

41

the occasional joint or drinking some beer on the weekend. Things like that. Not harmless, but not extreme either. There were kids in his school with more than enough parental supervision that had gotten into much worse activities and substances. Had Eugenio been too strict on him, Chuck may have never had a relationship with his high school sweetheart, Patty. When it came time to graduate, Patty was there on his arm. They walked across the stage in matching gowns and mortarboards. They had their first kiss at prom. Throughout all of that, Eugenio was there to applaud Chuck like a proud father. He never thought finding him in a garbage can all those years ago would lead to this.

Horace stops the story there. He knows Gigi could be with any guy she wants. The fame, money, and glamorous lifestyle intimidates him. So he believes that in finding out about who his father truly is, she'll question dating him. Much to Horace's surprise, however, Gigi is very receptive to this story. What Gigi cares most about more than anything in the world is sustainability, the idea of reducing, reusing, and recycling. Chuck, being salvaged from a trash can, made Horace the physical offspring of this ideology, which gives Horace an advantage over any other guy. Every time Gigi looks at him from now on, she's reminded of her passion. Horace's insecurity of inferiority does not understand that. But this is something that will stick in her mind no matter where she was.

Because his motive is to get off the topic as soon as possible, Horace digs into a picnic basket he prepared with plant-based meals and pulls out a couple of veggie burgers. Handing one over to Gigi, he asks a question, changing the topic away from his father.

"What does that cloud look like to you?" says Horace, unwrapping his burger.

"Oh my god, I love doing this. I'm such an Aries, I can't." Gigi looks to the sky and takes a nibble of her burger. "Mmmm! This veggie patty is life! Aww, see that little cloud over there? I feel bad for it. It's like, so lonely. It looks like he just wants a friend or something." Gigi points to a small cloud socially distanced away from a cluster of thick, epic, fluffy white clouds. "Oh my God, that's so sad I could literally die."

Horace giggles at Gigi's innocence, and they silently finish their veggie burgers while admiring the clouds. After a lovely afternoon of skygazing in the park, Horace walks Gigi back to her electric limousine. He builds up the nerve to kiss

43

her goodbye after opening the door for her. As the opaquely tinted window rolls up, Horace waves, and the limo drives off silently down the dusty road.

CHAPTER

The #DumpOff challenge is trending number one on Twitter. Because it's gone viral, the news makes the event into a block party held in town square. Pinky Mayes is victorious in the challenge. It's only by a pound or so, but it doesn't matter. If you win by a gram or a tonne, winning's winning. This means Mr. Disco and his garbage are put on display, making the main event a massive dunk tank where Michael's trash downpours on him anytime someone hits the bullseye from fifteen metres away. The tank is central to a plethora of funhouses, food trucks, megaphones blaring promises of magic, and carnival games. Children walk around smiling ear to ear, holding balloon animals and ice cream that drip on their light-up Sketchers. Carneys talk shit to men trying to win oversized teddy bears for their partners. Bernie is a victim to this feat while playing the ring toss. His wife fancies the big inflatable unicorn floaties. Bernie throws all his rings with precision but can't land a single one.

PING! The bottles ring as they bounce off the oversized necks like a pinball off a bumper. His attempts yield him shame and a twenty-dollar debt. They walk away and Bernie promises to buy her a floaty at the dollar store as they join the crowd moving towards the heart of the block party. Most adults can't pass up the opportunity to bury their local broadcaster. For a cash donation of whatever you can spare, you get three chances to crudely change Mr. Disco's forecast whilst supporting a meaningful cause. The charity of choice is wildlife protection for animals affected by the environmental damage caused by human sprawl.

Eugenio catches wind of this event and clears a part of his schedule for it. Nothing would bring him more joy than publicly and legally entombing one of his foes in their trash.

Michael is confident in the little garbage he produced, knowing it will be a light shower, especially after a few hours of locals throwing and missing the target. Michael thinks he's free and clear of this harmless humiliation, and the thousands of dollars raised for charity means it's shaping up to be a marvellous day for him and the community.

Everyone is happily nodding their heads to the music playing throughout the festival. As Michael is admiring this moment, he senses a change in the weather. Feint clouds screen the sun and the crowd parts for its next contestant who is brimming with confidence. Eugenio emerges from the clearing, pulling out a wad of cash held together by an elastic band from his perfectly pressed linens. He makes a more than generous donation, then grabs three beanbags. Setting the bullseye in sight, he walks to the throwing mark spray-painted on the cement. The mood shifts intensely and there is an intimidating silence among the crowd. The DJ for the event fades out the lively top forty music and starts to play harmonious introductory flutes from *The Good, The Bad and The Ugly*. This is officially a showdown. The only thing missing is a clock tower striking twelve times, signalling high noon.

Eugenio feels like a kid again. He thinks back to his little league days as a pitcher when his coach gave him the nickname 'The Bullet Train.' Looking at the ground, he puts one foot on the mark as if it were a pitching mound, squares up to the target, and raises the bean bag to his chin. In that moment, he pauses and looks up at Mr. Disco, who is staring him down. Eugenio starts his wind up and fires the bean bag right down the pipe.

THUD!

"Ooohh!" the crowd reacts with a low-pitched tone, like a third-grade classroom after one of the students gets sent to the office. Eugenio misses the target about five or six inches high, but everyone thought it was going to hit right on the money.

"Don't throw out your shoulder!" says Michael, laughing at his attempt.

Eugenio grins, using that to further motivate him. "Sit tight there, you Just For Men billboard. I hope you got an umbrella there."

It's casual banter, but deep down, Eugenio and Michael despise each other. Their interview on Channel Eight only made things worse. The crowd stays silent as Eugenio lines up for his next hurl. Tension fills the air like a lingering fart. Rolling his shoulders a couple of times, trying to grease his arthritic bones, Eugenio fires this one off quickly, in a less dramatic fashion, with a result no different than the first attempt. He picks up his final beanbag, closes his eyes, and remembers the 1981 little league finals.

It was a hot day and pressure was mounting. The pitcher called timeout and the coach walked over to the mound. After a quick meeting of the minds, they both made their way to the dugout as Eugenio got called in to close the game. His team, The Underdogs, had a narrow seven-to-six lead over their rivals, The Bombers. These two teams hated each other. The Bombers were all private school kids. As for the Underdogs, they were all lower class. This game was more of a battle between rich and poor than it was man versus man. The announcer came on over the speakers and addressed the crowd.

"Let me break it down for you folks. Bottom of the ninth, one out, runner on second. If you have a pacemaker or a weak stomach, you may need to call a doctor. Eugenio 'The Bullet Train' Violante is on his way to the mound. We are about to witness baseball in its purest form." Most pitchers would be nervous, but as a closer, Eugenio was used to this type of pressure. Calmly walking to the mound, he took a couple warm-up pitches, and the umpire resumed the game.

"Play ball!" he yelled, drawing the mask from his forehead down to his chin. The batter had no chance against his fastball, swinging and missing two pitches in a row, coming nowhere near making contact. The batter rooted his cleats into the dirt and gripped the bat tight. Sometimes you just have to close your eyes and hope for the best. Grip it and rip it. Eugenio fired a two-seamer right down the pipe. The batter managed to clip it just enough to have the ball bounce slowly down the first baseline. The batter sprinted toward first base as if his survival depended on it. Eugenio met him halfway down the line, bare handed the ball out of the dirt, and continued his momentum through the runner as he lowered his shoulder through their chest, dropping him to the ground. A bench-clearing brawl ensued. The announcer got out of his seat and went crazy.

"Eugenio just redefined charging the mound! That must be why they call him the bullet train! He's got a fastball like a red eye to Tokyo and hits you like a locomotive!"

Meanwhile, jerseys were being torn, punches were being thrown, sand was being kicked, and 'fuck yous' were being handed out like bad grades in summer school. The batter on deck sprinted toward Eugenio and cross-checked him to the ground with a Louisville slugger. Eugenio had never had the wind knocked out of him like that before. He laid on his back, witnessing the battle for a few moments. Both teams were mercifully separated by their coaches, and the dust settled from the chaos. The Bombers' head coach was Michael's father, and he was not happy with the violence Michael just displayed.

"Stop being an idiot kid! You go out there and you win us the game. Otherwise, I take that new Atari your mother got you and I give it to someone who deserves it." His dad gave him a stern talk before the umpire regained control of the game and Eugenio caught his breath. Everyone headed back to their positions. The previous play had allowed the runner on second to advance to third base during the commotion. The final batter stepped up to the plate, swinging his bat confidently, the same player that had knocked the wind out of Eugenio. The announcer began to build suspense.

"This could be the ball game! Michael Disco takes to the plate as he looks for his second dinger of the game. And boy oh boy, what a walk-off it would be." This was the first time Eugenio and Michael had ever faced off. It was the beginning of a life-long rivalry. Eugenio, still upset from Michael's brawling tactics, fired a warning shot, whipping a fastball that skimmed his nose before Michael fell to the ground, dodging it startlingly.

"Ball!" the umpire screamed quickly. Michael

stood in for the next pitch. Eugenio fired it in the same spot.

"Ball two!" yelled the umpire again. The tension built as the showdown continued. After a couple of deep foul balls, it would come down to the final pitch. Three balls, two strikes, game on the line. The catcher gave Eugenio the signal and he threw the ball over the plate. While everyone was expecting another heater, Eugenio threw a nasty, off-speed curveball. A family of ducks could have crossed the road by the time this ball crossed home plate. Michael's mistimed swing only caught air.

"Sti-riiiike three!" the umpire yelled dramatically. Michael stared down Eugenio deviously as hats flew off in celebration. Cheering reigned from all corners of the diamond while arbitration was ordered by the Bombers' head coach. Michael looked up to his dad in disappointment, hoping for endearment while he argued the call. Instead, he was crushed by his father's resentment and anger. The hometown heroes dogpiled the pitcher's mound while their rivals bowed their heads in defeat. It was an intense battle of the classes. A victory for the lower class meant everything to them.

Eugenio opens his eyes and channels that moment. Everybody was trying to hit the target as hard as they could, missing wildly. So he takes a deep breath, with time slowing as he exhales. Hurling the beanbag forward, Eugenio curves it right through the bullseye. No hats fly off in celebration this time, but Mr. Disco's humiliation is more rewarding than any trophy. Behind the scenes, Eugenio made sure to send in his associates to add some grubby items to Michael's load of trash: a few rotten scaly fishes, curdled dairy, and a couple of pints of red paint for good measure. As the garbage showers Michael, his hairpiece comes loose and ends up on top of the waste pile. The crowd is silent, shocked by Michael's newfound cul-de-sac hairline. Covered in red paint, except for his pale, shiny crown, Michael nervously farts. Michael's tighty-whities thud to his ankles after being filled with a fresh dookie. The crowd continues to be shocked in silence. A defeated and now bald Michael Disco bows his head in defeat the same way he did in 1981.

The following day, Channel Eight News' top story is the block party, showing videos from TikTok of everyone pouring garbage on their friends and family. The last video shown is a hairless Michael Disco standing in a pile of filth. Someone had made a techno remix using his fart as the beat. It is surprisingly catchy.

"Don't feel bad, Michael. Look at all the money we raised!" Pinky says reassuringly. The movement raised hundreds of thousands of dollars across the globe.

After the success of the fundraiser, the streets are ready for Eugenio's upgrade. The new collection vehicles had been dropped off and a select few were trained on how to use them properly. Eugenio is excited. This truly is a revolutionary idea. He doesn't spend much time on the business end of Wastefellas, as it's more of a front for his gambling operations, but this leering issue against the company is unprecedented. The fewer eyes looking at him the better.

At eight o'clock the next morning, all autonomous garbage vehicles set off into the public. Eugenio knows the people are going to love it. Every neighbourhood has their phones out to record as they come by, praising how much more silent the electric motors are. No more ground-shaking vibrations as the vehicle approached your home like an Apache full of wild rhinos was about to land on your lawn. No more polluted diesel fumes and smoke left behind. As the weeks go on, social media is buzzing. The public is genuinely happy for a moment in time. And in that time, Eugenio lives in a rare juncture of peace.

Eugenio can finally get back to business as usual. His officially organized but officially illegal poker games are the biggest earners. After weeks of laying low, the dormant, seemingly abandoned building these games take place in can re-open. However, it has to operate differently now. No more sketchy, late-night cash pickups and drop-offs. The new autonomous technology developed for Wastefellas doubles as a way of transporting the cash a lot easier. Nobody has to be there. All it requires is taking out the trash. The money is gathered in garbage bags and collected by the vehicles without raising an eyebrow. And worst-case scenario, if the vehicle has been compromised by any authorities, Eugenio has plausible deniability that it ever happened. Plausible deniability is the best type of deniability. What are they going to do? Lock up a robot for breaking the law? A prison for artificially intelligent robotic criminals may be possible in the future, but decommissioning these vehicles right now would put the town back to where it started. Not to mention Eugenio's insurance policy pays the crooked cops weekly. They sacrifice their morals to make quick riches and have his protection. So the cash drops smoothly operate on a regular schedule.

They move around a lot of money. And wherever there's money, there's going to be problems. One night as they're transporting their cash like any other night, the vehicle suddenly veers on a different route. The crew monitoring the autonomous transaction is confused as to why. Whenever they reprogram the destination, nothing changes. Attempting to switch from autopilot to manual controls fails as well. Referring to the manual, they're instructed to remotely shut down the vehicle — it's likely there's a malfunction with the software. Mercifully, the command is received. Having such a large sum of cash like a sitting duck in the middle of the street is risky. So one of the engineers volunteers to drive over with Jimmy and sort the whole situation out. The rest of the team stay to monitor the location. To their surprise, the vehicle is showing that it is still on the move. However, it is no longer abiding by the safety codes and sensors that govern it. The vehicle is on an all-out midnight joyride, drifting, dancing, and speeding in a maniacal circle. They aren't sure if the screen is accurately displaying the vehicle's movements. But to be safe, they call Jimmy and make him drive the doors off his Buick to the scene. After turning the corner on the street where it's located, Jimmy confirms their worst fears. It's completely out of control.

Typically, the mob has a way of making their problems disappear. A stern threat usually does the trick, or the classic, throw a hand grenade in their competitor's business at two in the morning and set the building on fire. But that's the old-school mentality. That's for when you know who your enemy is. Their problem in the new era is something they did not foresee: hackers or 'hacktivists.' It could be anyone, anywhere, anytime. Somebody had been monitoring their cash drops and had slowly penetrated their network. So they were able to log on and take control midway through the route. The only problem was that a glitch in the system was triggered when more than one server was logged in at the same time. So when they shut down the power, it locked both parties from controlling the collection vehicle. However, it did not shut down the communication to the CPU. Which is why the vehicle is acting like some sort of rabid robot. Its brain is frying while it operates at maximum capacity.

Jimmy yells at the engineer in a panic to try to stop the machine, but there's nothing that can be done. This autonomous Godzilla can only be stopped by blowing it up. Jimmy heads to his trunk, pulls out a rifle, and feeds it ten pounds of lead, shooting out the tires and shredding through the hardware. In a last-ditch effort, the vehicle flies up a curb, and Jimmy snipes a kill shot in the battery while spinning through mid-air. The vehicle explodes as bullets penetrate the sparking short circuits. When it lands on the opposite side of the fenced road, all that can be seen is fire and thick smoke. Sprinting to the other side, Jimmy is presented with three things: a vehicle lying on the street in a ball of fire, flaming bills of cash raining softly overtop of the scene, and a dead body. Jimmy acts as fast as he can to cover it up. But it's too late. The noise has woken up everyone in the neighbour-hood. Crowds of tired, nosey, and zombie-like neighbours start to flood the streets in their robes and pyjamas. Sirens from fire trucks approach. Worst of all, Nigel Dansby is approaching in his white news van. Jimmy starts to feel the butterflies flutter in his stomach. He doesn't see a way out of this one. There would be no coming back from another negative news story on Wastefellas Garbage Co. It could be the end of the company. Regardless, Jimmy scurries to the wreckage and tries to hide the incriminating evidence. The engineer takes all the cash back to Jimmy's Buick and drives away like he's about to be late for his daughter's piano recital. Jimmy, back at the crash, is now on his own, coming to terms with the reality of his future. Racking up a third-degree murder charge with an unregistered rifle is not something he can foresee getting away with. Every idea Jimmy has that sparks some sort of escape is met almost immediately with the common denominator of the situation. Somebody had lost their life. There is no saving the contorted and dismembered man under the flaming vehicle. And it only gets worse as more and more people gather around the blaze. Jimmy had taken care of the most important part of the situation at hand: cash. It's on its way to safety. Jimmy, however, is far from freedom. Slowly accepting his fate, the time comes for him to pay his dues, both to the mafia and to the universe. Naturally in his line of work, you are apt to build a mountain of bad karma. In times of despair, Jimmy shuts off his emotions and numbs himself as a coping mechanism. Standing alone, he looks about his surroundings as new activities begin to unfold, repeating the blood oath he took when he was sworn into the mob over and over in his head.

You must never betray any of the secrets of this Cosa Nostra. You must never violate the wife or children of another member. You must never become involved with narcotics.

Nigel and his crew quickly set up in front of Jimmy's autonomous purgatory. With burrows of smoke, flashing sirens, and the occasional hundred-dollar bill floating down in flames, the frame is set and he starts to report.

"A fatal collision occurred late tonight. Known assailant to the mob, Jimmy Biraghi, is being questioned by the public behind me and is most likely responsible for the death of the unidentified victim."

Nigel moves in closer to the crash site as commotion rises. The presumed mother of the victim is keeled over and crying uncontrollably, pointing toward Mr. Biraghi. Jimmy feels bad for what happened. But his numbness won't allow him to respond or show any emotion to her. The underdressed community slowly moves towards Jimmy as they notice the dead body. Multiple people start to jostle him. Jimmy pushes back. The only emotion Jimmy cannot numb is anger. So once the crowd gets physical, he pushes back. The horde starts overwhelming him. In a last effort to stop the riot, Jimmy pulls his pistol and fires warning shots into the air.

BANG! BANG!

Silence dawns, except for the weeping mother. Jimmy stands with his pistol pointed at an eager crowd.

"My baby!" screams out the weeping mother into the night. Nigel has footage of the whole scenario. Their frame holds as so: Jimmy points his handgun into the silent and motionless crowd. Smoke blows in the wind in front of an inferno next to a devastated mother.

"Get him!" One person charges Jimmy like an urban Braveheart. Jimmy fires into him until his magazine runs out. The trigger clicks as he pulls it back over and over. Without a loaded weapon. The wall of people charges at him. Jimmy throws his gun and charges back. Upon impact, Jimmy disappears into the mouth of the horde as the footage cuts to censored SMPTE colour bars.

Bleeeeeeeeeeeeeeeeeeeeeeeeeeeeeeeeeeeep.

CHAPTER

Three Months Later...

It's the ninety-day anniversary of the declaration of civil war. Conditions for residents in the town start to reach their expiration date. Food isn't as abundant anymore, the streets are filled with garbage, and nature has begun to nestle a new home in once bustling areas. Leaving your house is no longer considered a joyous occasion, but more of an expedition to gather precious provisions.

On the other side of town, Wastefellas Garbage Co fortunately offers its headquarters as a shelter for its employees and their families. Eugenio is a violent man, but when it comes to family and friends, he never spares a nickel. Sleeping arrangements can only be described as military. But there are no other options for slumber. They make it work as best they can. Conditions are surely forgiven whenever it is time to eat. Eugenio would never have the people he cares about heating no-name cans or Chef Boyardee. Every day the menu is catered by Eugenio's family. An example of his culinary elegance offered to the people consists of a lemon chicken piccata served with veal and charred broccolini one night for dinner. He makes sure, at the very least, the women and children are taken care of. The perimeter is also guarded at all times by heavily armed mobsters. Everyone knows not to go near there unless they want a lead shower. Alienated like Area 51, the mobsters and sanitation workers must act as a team to find their way out of this.

The experienced group of mechanics has been preparing a blueprint of modifications. Most of them have been working on anything with an engine and wheels since childhood. So it doesn't take long before they have the schematics mapped for an all-out war-mongering machine. Phase one is the most important: armouring and bullet-proofing the truck. This means steel beams to reinforce the frame, doors, and windows; giant off-road, run-flat tires that can run over anything and keep on rolling; not to mention a one-tonne cowcatcher welded to the front end for throwing obstacles out of its track. Phase two mandates some upgraded engine components and suspension. A beefed-up turbocharger, open exhaust, and simple tune are all they need to have some extra power. You can't have an off-road machine without a snorkel intake for any battles taking place in water. This upgrade is highly functional, but mainly they like it because it gives a badass presence. Not that it wasn't badass already. On top of that, they'll stiffen the shocks a little and raise the ride height a few inches. Phase three is weapons: carve out a manhole in the roof above the passenger seat for a turret to be mounted and fit the front rims with sharp steel spikes capable of cutting through anything short of a Douglas fir. Once all the details are sorted out, the guys head into the workshop with dozens of garbage trucks to prepare. Late into the night and early into the morning, the mechanics tinker and clank on their heavy machinery working in shifts so they can rest properly. It's only step one, converting these garbage trucks into garbage tanks. From there they must pilot them into the streets and put their work on the frontline.

Another night of dinner dawns. On this day, there is a buzz about the now-established colony. The professionally untrained family goes for a classic service: chicken parmesan with a timeless ragu. Eugenio's mother's hands are gold when it comes to grain. However, arthritis prevents her from crafting her flawless linguine. So Chuck's wife, Patty, offers to be her ox in the kitchen. She mentors Patty on the gentle ballet that is carefully mixing the yolks and kneading the finely milled farina. They spend hours stretching the dough to the perfect thickness before cutting the lightly dusted sheets. Extra virgin olive oil, crushed tomatoes, garlic, and a touch of basil are all the accoutrements needed for handmade pasta. Boiling the linguine just until it floats and plating that with Mario's chicken parmigiana is one of the most beautiful meals ever to bless a piece of porcelain. Most families here weren't even eating this well in their own homes before the war. And after a tidal wave of carbs, a well-timed food coma made their Navy Seal sleeping arrangements more than tolerable.

Due to the scarcity of space, families within the close quarters start getting to know each other a little more. Horace is introduced to all of the sons and daughters of Chuck's co-workers. They get along surprisingly well, although Horace is missing Gigi, thinking he'll never see her again. Meeting Reggie's cousin, Carmen, gives him a new burst of energy. Just blossoming into her nineteenth birthday, Carmen and Horace were accepted into the same environmental engineering program, which they initially bond over. They are attracted to each other on many levels, not just physical. The first day they meet, time flies by. Both are interested in the environment because of their families and growing up hearing their fathers talk about how much waste they throw away daily, how it occupies the landfill like a bad tenant. They share ideas on how to make the world a better place. Carmen has an Instagram business where she makes jewellery out of recycled materials. Horace has a grand plan to create an app to help people monitor their carbon footprint. He feels that being more aware by tracking such a thing could begin to change the mindset of the masses. As Horace and Carmen continue with their conversation, preparations are concluding for an ambush on the town.

The landfill is separated by a backroad that intersects with the highway just a few kilometres up. After the highway is the danger zone. That's where the town limits established a blockade. Most likely, that is where their first point of contact will happen. After some preparations, a fleet of trucks leaves the compound to patrol the streets. What the public has in numbers, the garbage workers have in artillery. These seemingly impenetrable vehicles are surely no match for the weapons of the locals. This war is comparable to the battle of Thermopylae, more commonly known as the Battle of 300, vastly outnumbered by soldiers, but highly superior in skill.

Armed guards at the perimeter gates salute them as they exit the safety of their asylum. The gates close behind the trucks — there is no going back. Chuck, leading the pack, is silent, but his radio screams a face-melting guitar solo. Reggie, air guitaring the lick while head-banging, is loosening up for bloodshed. Most of the crew is angry and nervous. Is this the only way? History has never favoured war as the solution to conflict. Yet time and time again, we find ourselves at war with each other. Divided. Chuck's thoughts completely disappear after hearing some locals fire a few warning shots to the sky.

"We goin' to war, dawg! Are there any rules we need to know? We need to be shot at to do something, or can I just start poppin'?" Reggie asks.

"There are no rules, Reggie. This is war. Just survive." Chuck squints, looking ahead. There is a massive blockade. He continues his tense response to Reggie as more bullets fly over the truck. "Just don't hesitate. Hesitation will get you killed." Preparing for contact, Chuck grabs his radio.

"Truck two, truck three. Do you copy?" Chuck says, testing his communications.

"Roger, cap'n. Attila the Hung, ready for combat," replies one truck with their self-proclaimed codename.

"Loud and clear, captain. If we're doing penis codenames, I wanna be Plymouth Rockhard. Over," replies the other truck.

"Alright, dipshits, pull up beside me. We're running through this barricade side by side. Engage," Chuck relays to the trucks behind him.

They line up in arrangement as they approach the barricade. It's a large barricade, about fourteen or fifteen feet high, blocking the entire intersection. Since nobody is around to collect the trash, the town has used it to block the entrance from the highway. It's difficult to see over. Besides the occasional bullet, it is silent, and no one is in the streets. All trucks redline the throttle. The turbines emit a high-pitched spooling sound as their speed climbs. They crash through piles of garbage. Materials caught by the cowcatchers helicopter in every direction. The sharp steel blades coming off the wheels cut deep through the base of the blockade like a first breakup. The pure mass of the trucks shatters through the roadblock with ease.

"Woooohoooo!" one truck driver yells through the radio. Just then, gunfire rains from the rooftops.

"Contact!" All co-pilots climb to the turret and shred through the building. Everyone on the roof ducks for cover. The turrets take a moment to reload as a secondary team comes from the ground floor of the building. Their rifles might as well have been Super Soakers. The fleet of armoured trucks is untouched. Once the turrets are reloaded, the ground team is annihilated within seconds. Melting through the base of the building even further, the snipers on the rooftops are buried by the structure as it collapses on itself. The townspeople are like a praying mantis to a silverback gorilla.

In the distance is a second barricade — trash bags piled meters high. That seems to be their first choice in the line of defence. Everyone gets out of the truck, looting the bodies for more weapons and ammunition. Afterwards, the corpses are thrown into the back of the truck's hopper, suffering the same fate as their waste: clawed, compressed, and crushed into a paste. Even though they were reprimanded by the people, the crew, at heart, is still committed to keeping the streets clean when possible. As they go through the area making sure nobody has survived, Chuck takes a bullet to the shoulder and drops to the ground. Crawling to cover, he commands the rest of the crew.

"I'm hit! Everybody in the truck!" Reggie runs over to help Chuck as he dodges enemy fire. "In the truck, Reggie! Take out the next roadblock, and don't let them move in on us! I'll be fine."

Chuck pulls out his medi pack and assesses the wound. The bullet went straight through. He painfully applies pressure and tapes it back up with some gauze. Up ahead, Chuck hears the squad crash through the next barrier while simultaneously opening fire, bringing a demented smile to his face. Chuck takes advantage of his adrenaline and sprints into an unoccupied building until the road clears. With his gun drawn, he slowly approaches a blinking light in the back. To his delight, an 'Rx' sign is flickering sporadically. Looting the ibuprofen and amphetamines, Chuck pops a few pills and makes his way up the road now that the shooting has ceased. Still, though, Chuck is moving carefully, staying low and next to cover the whole time. In between the trucks ahead and himself, Gigi is standing over her bodyguard. He is bleeding out while mouthing his last words to her.

"Gigi. You have the power to end this." The bodyguard coughs up blood amidst his sentence. "You can save the world," he says with little energy as his lips turn blue and his face becomes paler. Gigi holds him as he lies motionless. Chuck approaches them silently. As Gigi loses focus of her surroundings, Chuck pounces. Pointing his gun at the bodyguard for a moment, Chuck grabs Gigi and runs to the rally point a block away. Reggie hears him running towards them.

"Chuck, what the fuck are you doing? That's definitely not in the rules."

There is no time for debate. Chuck needs to drive back to the compound and secure his newfound prisoner of war. "I already told you, Reggie, there are no fuckin' rules. You want to win this war, you gotta fight dirty."

Chuck hops in the truck and peels out. Reggie joins with the rest of the crew and brings them up to speed.

Chuck, approaching the compound quickly, signals the guard. Waved through the opening gates, Chuck brings the truck to the workshop and unloads the precious cargo. Chuck wraps Gigi in a blanket and discreetly escorts her around the back of the compound to a room where she can be contained. To her surprise, she scouts a familiar face along the way: Horace. He's sitting outside having a picnic with Carmen. Jealousy and confusion fill her stomach. Just as she looks away, Horace turns in her direction. He cannot recognize her but is excited to see his dad back from conflict. Before long, Gigi is locked in the same room Chuck was raised in. Leaving her a plate of focaccia and espresso, Chuck makes his way to Eugenio.

"Hey uh, Eugenio. I gotta show you something. C'mon. Follow me." Chuck leads him to the tucked-away office room and opens the door.

"Holy... Shit. Chuck, you're off the fuckin' richter!" Eugenio is shocked. Initially, he is angry at Chuck for kidnapping her. But as Chuck explains the bargaining position this gives them, his emotions plateau. "How is the rest of the crew? Are they okay?"

"They're fine. I'm proud of them. Those boys are war machines. We established a good position in the town before I left. Reggie will lead them heroically," says Chuck reassuringly. Eugenio and Chuck head back to the compound, keeping the kidnapping on the hush-hush. As they leave, Horace comes in the other door to hug his dad. Instead, he is greeted with a cold, empty room.

Reggie and the gang are patrolling the streets in the active area of operation. They have a stronghold in the area. Nobody wants to go near them after hearing stories of being thrown in the back of the loader and being converted to pulled pork or being assaulted by a barrage of incendiary bullets blowing organs out of people's backs while they're on fire.

With Tupac blaring, the thug life is starting to take over. Reggie decides to loot the liquor store. He shoots out a window and starts rummaging through bottles of booze. Old English is what he first has in mind. It gets you drunk the fastest and prepares you for battle, be it with yourself or the general public. Either way, a forty is an economy-class ticket to some quality demon time, perfect for war, but this isn't a trench war. This is a war where they are in command. The social class pyramid is flipped on its head. Now garbage workers are kings. So instead of a bottle of Boone's Farm or Fireball whiskey, coming out of the liquor boutique, Reggie hands out bottles of Pauillac red to everyone, a five-thousand-dollar cabernet sauvignon in one hand and a three-hundred-dollar Glock in the other.

The boys are getting ignorant, listening to Pusha T while looking for enemies. Reggie finds the funniest thing he could imagine right on schedule. Gary. Wearing a cloak and standing in the middle of a flickering streetlight, holding a replica Darth Maul lightsaber. The humming sound of contained energy pulses softly across the quiet dawn. Reggie tells everyone to stop. He gets out with a baseball bat and yells at Gary.

"I'm gonna fuck you up, Gary! Cross-eyed bitch!" Now, everyone knows Gary is cross-eyed, but his astigmatism is unique. Gary isn't east to west cross-eyed like you would typically see. Gary is reverse cross-eyed. North to south cross-eyed. Meaning he can see an aeroplane fly right over him and tell you what colour your Yeezy's are at the same time, without moving his head. Reggie stands ten paces from Gary as they stare each other down.

"It's over, Anakin!" screams Gary in a British accent.

Reggie laughs and gives Gary the chance to flee. "Ay yo, Gary! You can leave now, and we won't kill you. Seriously, man, it doesn't feel right hitting you with your eyes like that."

"NO! The force is strong within me!" Gary raises his lightsaber as the flickering light above him burns out. He charges Reggie. "Ahhhhhhh!" Screaming with rage he swings his mighty light-saber. *Schvrmmmmmmmm!*

"Umm … Gary … I'm over here," says Reggie, standing about six feet to the side. Gary's depth perception doth fooled him. "For real, Gary, we into some bad shit. Just get outta here, man."

"Never!" Gary screams with pride. He charges Reggie again, this time actually in line with him.

"Ahhhhhhh!" Reggie laughs as he comes towards him and swings his bat through the scale model lightsaber, thinking the charades will end. But upon impact, his bat gets sliced in half as the lightsaber beams through it. *Kwishuuuuuuuuuu!*

Everyone's jaw drops.

"What the fuck? This motha fucka got a real ass lightsaber!" Gary takes another swing at Reggie. This time he is much more cautious. Ducking under the blow, Reggie runs back to his truck and gets in.

"Stay out my trash, boy! I told you I'd git ya for that one!" Gary says, retracting his lightsaber and disappearing into the night.

"Dude has a full-on plasma cutter! That shit almost had me fucked up! Electrons, protons, neutrons, wontons, croutons, all that shit!" Reggie says to the driver with his heart beating through his chest.

"Fuck! I told you! Magnetic fields and shit ain't nothin' to play with! All those batteries and magnets in his trash. Gary is a cross-eyed Jedi! Fucked up! I'm callin' Chuck. He's gotta hear this shit."

Back at the compound, Horace hears a chair scrape the floor and approaches it, thinking Chuck is just looking for some peace. Instead, he finds Gigi being held prisoner.

"Gigi?! How did you get here?" Horace says with surprise.

"Don't act like you care, Horace. I saw you with another girl. That guy brought me in here. He smelled like feet," responds a sassy Gigi. Horace starts to put the pieces together.

"That guy who smells like feet is my dad," Horace says regretfully. "When I told you the story of my dad, I never told you he ended up working for Wastefellas. I didn't want to tell you. I thought it would make you resent me. I'm sorry, Gigi. I should have been honest with you." Horace feels a ball in his throat build.

Gigi gives him the death stare and responds. "Your dad is a dick! But you're so sweet. I'm mad!

But I want a hug." Horace approaches cautiously and extends his arms to Gigi as an alarm sounds.

BLILILILILING!

CHAPTER

Eugenio, standing off to the side, activates the alarm after Chuck receives Reggie's call. They develop an action plan. It includes more fighting and destruction. However, tonight at midnight would be the finale. Eugenio and Chuck round up all available soldiers. They all take a moment to say a heartfelt goodbye to their families, promising to return. Lengthy goodbye 'airport hugs' are bestowed among loved ones. One last moment of silent appreciation is shown. Everyone heads to their trucks, ready to re-enter the warzone.

On the way to meeting Reggie in the town square, a convoy of garbage warriors obnoxiously disturb the silence of the night, passing by crumbled buildings, overgrown foliage, miles of trash, and maliciously dismembered body parts spread across the blood-stained streets. The view is awful, and the smell transcends their ill stomachs. Before long, everyone has convened at the town square. Eugenio, leading the convoy, greets Reggie. He and his crew are drunk, armed to the tits, and gathered around a fire constructed of residual trash. The plan of action is simple. Everyone takes a sector of the town and relays their message through the trucks' PA systems. A variation of this message is communicated repeatedly.

"Every household will send one soldier to the town square. The final battle will conclude our conflict. If nobody is to show up, we will take out everyone including the women and children. The battle begins at midnight."

As for Reggie and his crew, their message is delivered much less accurately. The boys are still wasted off red wine, drinking, driving, and swerving around their sector.

"Free cookies in the town square!" yells the driver in a British accent. The crew's laughs bleed through the intercom. "Pshshhshh! Town square! Free oranges and ice cream sundaes! It's gonna be super fun!" says the driver, laughing uncontrollably and breaking his newly adopted royal family cadence. He passes Reggie the microphone and encourages him to give it a try.

For the next hour, all the town hears are the messages repeated over and over again. Eventually, the mayor hears the totalitarian echoes and decides he needs to act on it. Like most families at the time, he is nestled safely away in his home. But he breaches that safety, not only because he promised to provide leadership to the town, but he also heard promises of free cookies.

The mayor arrives early to the town square, partly in hopes of striking a deal before the massacre begins, partly because he wants to get there before they run out of cookies. Eugenio shakes hands with him and they enter the town hall. Obviously, this issue is the height of the township's priority, which warrants the use of the primary boardroom. The centrepiece is a beautiful, five-metre-long Victorian table hand-crafted from solid walnut and surrounded by baroque pillars and intricate crown mouldings. The antique watercolour landscape paintings reflect the light illuminated by an exquisite crystal chandelier glistening ever so slightly. The mayor takes a seat at one end of the table, and Eugenio faces him on the opposite side.

The mayor opens negotiations offensively. "First things first. Where are the cookies?"

"What the hell are you talking about?" Eugenio says, unaware of Reggie and his crew's false, drunken promises of dessert.

"I've been eating Alphaghetti for three months! I heard cookies, and I want a damn cookie!" says the mayor, slamming his fist into the walnut tabletop.

"Okay, calm down, guy. We'll get you some cookies after this is all over," Eugenio says, settling the mayor down.

The mayor continues on saying Eugenio's men need to leave town. Eugenio doesn't want war, but he isn't going to comply with any authority. The people rose up against something. It inspired Eugenio that everyone had come together. It just so happened they picked a fight with the wrong people. The irony of the situation stimulates Eugenio's brain.

"The public is only fighting themselves. We are not the problem. Sure, we aren't perfect. But we are not the problem. I agree with what the people are saying. I just don't agree with the direction of their fingers or the gavel they strike. I agree with the wastefulness. We raised a child, a child I found in a dumpster, mind you. We raised that child with almost nothin' but trash from the landfill.

We cleaned up clothes, repaired broken furniture, pumped up old tires, and we gave that kid everything he needed," Eugenio says to the mayor in a philosophic moment.

"Eugenio, this all got out of hand so quickly. For Christ's sake, look around! We've been protesting pollution for the last year, and now we're living in it. Something needs to be done to stop the battle at midnight," the mayor says as the clock ticks closer to zero hour.

Outside of their meeting, the domestic soldiers begin to gather. On the east side of the square stands an overwhelming sea of locals wielding much less destructive weaponry than Wastefellas' counterparts. They hold typical things you might find around the household like garden shears, golf clubs, shovels, hammers, slingshots, crossbows, and basic firearms. One hopeful grandmother wields a wooden spoon confidently. These are all things that can be acquired legally. Many of the town's handymen are proud to showcase more complex ordinances, such as DIY variants of flamethrowers. One person uses the power of a leaf blower combined with fuel injectors and gasoline. Another more basic version combines Axe body spray and a Bic lighter. Then you have a group of guys filling up Molotov cocktails and another group sharpening javelins made from wrought iron gate posts. Some people are still whacking rusty nails into their Louisville sluggers. It looks like a sea of military MacGyvers. The most popular of the illegal weapons is a close tie between brass knuckles, bear mace, and homemade tasers made from disposable cameras. When you put all of them together, it looks as though there is hope, not only that they can win the battle, but that they can be resourceful.

On the west side of the square stands a mixed bag of sanitation workers and Mafioso-type gentlemen with a hankering for violence. Not too many of them, however — maybe around a hundred. But when you compare the weapons, it feels like numbers won't matter. The sanitation workers have turrets mounted on top of their bulletproof trucks. They have military-grade assault rifles. And they have enough rocket-propelled grenade launchers to give the fourth of July her period early.

Standing atop one of the few remaining buildings, overlooking the square, is Michael Disco. He takes this opportunity not to defend his town, but to document a news story that could skyrocket his career, going from a locally recognizable anchorman to a Geraldo Rivera-type sensation. Knowing the impact this could have on his career, Michael grows nervous. So he rubs some cocaine around his gums for a little inspiration and ironically, to calm his nerves. He sets up a tripod while the gathering of soldiers readies for battle in the frame underneath him.

Clearing his nose, he begins. "Hello everybody. I'm Michael Disco. The environmental apocalypse has reached a tipping point in this town, and tonight marks the dawn of a new era — a sustainable era."

The time is 11:58. Two minutes to battle. The civilians of the town stand facing their opposition. One of the locals steps forward and turns to his comrades.

"The garbage industry has divided us as a people. They pollute our planet and demand we give them a break. Well, the world is burning alive! And tonight, we burn with it!" He screams, raising a nine iron into the air. Pacing back and forth, he continues a very inspirational speech. "Tonight, we fight without mercy!"

The crowd of thousands of warriors screams in unison. An overwhelming roar spikes the adrenaline of everyone nearby. A conch horn starts to blow in the distance, innately signalling the beginning of a barbaric battle. They all blitz forward, proudly brandishing their weapons.

"Ahhhggghhhhhhhhhhhh!" Every soldier charges toward the sanitation's artillery. It is difficult to determine whether this is a revolution or a rebellion. The town has been so misled by the media. They blame the sanitation workers for the waste they are creating, ignorantly labelling themselves revolutionists. Blind unity and anger bind this special group of people to a historic moment. This moment truly will change the future of sustainability, but they aren't aware of that. They believe the people they employ to collect their garbage are the ones to blame. Unwilling to back down, they continue their push.

"Yeaaaaghhhhhhhhhh!" the crowd roars louder and louder.

Inside the town hall, Eugenio flexes his position as Gigi's captor. The mayor can hear the thunderous outcry as the crusade begins. Every second he hesitates to give Eugenio what he wants—freedom for the sanitation workers and his associates—the mayor sacrifices lives. And every moment the negotiations continue, Eugenio's hand gains strength. The mayor has to swallow his pride and adhere to Eugenio's terms, not only for his town, but for the hostiles and refugees created by the partition.

A final handshake is transferred, and the mayor hopes to stop the anarchy immediately.

Meanwhile, the sanitation enterprise fires into the crowd barrelling towards them. There is not a single bullet that doesn't meet a target. They unload every shot in their extended clips for what feels like minutes. More and more bodies are piling up as the onslaught of firepower shreds through the so-called revolutionists. When the time comes to reload, grenades and rocket launchers are sent into the nucleus of the crowd. Hundreds of explosives sequentially detonate across the entire square. One explosion after another elevates bodies and pavement into the heavens and crashes the surrounding structures to Earth. The blasts eventually lead to a halt after an excessive spree. Heavy smoke and dust clouds everyone's visibility. No one is able to see more than a foot ahead of them. As it settles, a crater is slowly exposed. There is no one left. All is silent.

A few of the garbage workers decide to observe the damage up close. They silently walk in and around the crater. Amidst their ringing ears, the only sounds are boots sinking into loose gravel and the occasional cascade of rocks tumbling into the crater. Chuck sees his reflection through a shattered piece of glass from the town landmark. He takes a good look at himself, reflecting on the trauma this whole situation has brought him. An impulsive thought causes Chuck to raise a gun to his head, staring intensely at his reflection in silence. At that moment, a noise breaks his concentration, and Chuck spins around quickly.

It is Michael Disco digging his way out of the rubble. The building he had been reporting on collapsed during the onslaught. Michael cannot believe his luck, surviving the demolition virtually unscathed. Rising out of the debris, he dusts himself off. Chuck doesn't believe his eyes. Now, having just escaped death, the only thing between Michael and his safety is an armed Chuck, who raises his gun towards Michael as Michael's arms fly up in shock.

"It's over, Chuck! Lower your gun!" Michael's plea echoes through the gallows of destruction while Chuck remains silent. "Please!" Michael pleads one more time.

"It's never over Michael. Not as long as you're here." Michael stares at Chuck in confusion and hopelessness. "Don't you get it? You're the conductor of this chaos, Michael. You aired my video on the news! You turned the people against the blue-collar garbage workers! *You* did this!" Chuck regains the squirrely eyed gaze he gave Bernie on that day before this all started—the gaze of a man on the edge, about to crack.

"I was doing my job, Chuck! You can't put that on me! I just read a teleprompter," Chuck responds to Michael immediately.

"Shut up!" Chuck screams.

"The #DumpOff wasn't even my idea. It was Pinky! I'm the one who was humiliated in front of everybody!"

Chuck laughs. "Oh yeah. I remember that," Chuck says, giggling to himself. He begins to laugh hysterically. "I heard you shit your pants!" Chuck is now laughing uncontrollably.

"I'm not the guy you're after, Chuck! I'm just the messenger!"

Chuck is still laughing madly. After regaining seriousness, he responds, "One of us has to go, Michael. That's just the way it has to be." Chuck is now holding the gun back up to Michael.

As Eugenio and the mayor open the large doors of the town hall leading to the main steps of the plaza, they are presented by an execution in the making. Michael Disco is kneeling in front of an unhinged Chuck. With his hands raised in the air, he pleads for his life.

"Please, Chuck! I can leave town. You'll never see me again."

Chuck grips the gun firmly. "What do you think would be a good headline, Michael? Good evening, everyone! This is news reporter Michael Disco! Tonight's top story: Disco Fever Dies!" says Chuck with a smirk on his face, mimicking Michael in a patronizing tone.

"That's pretty good actually. But no! There doesn't need to be a headline. There doesn't need to be a story! Let me go and everything will go back to normal. Please," pleads Michael, knowing this will be his last cry for help.

"There's no such thing as normal, Michael." Chuck firmly squeezes his weapon as Michael closes his eyes.

Eugenio screams from the crest of the town hall steps. "Chuck! It's over. Put the gun down."

Michael looks atop the stairs. With the moonlight dawning over Eugenio and the town hall, Michael believes he is listening to an angel. Chuck looks to Eugenio and argues his case.

"C'mon! Let me take him out! Look what he did to us! Look what he caused!" Chuck is on the edge of breaking. The only person he would listen to at this point was Eugenio, someone he considered to be a father figure his whole life, somebody whose advice was good as gold to him.

"He didn't cause anything, Chuck. There is nobody to blame. Shit, there's nobody *left* to blame because we killed half the fuckin' town. So put the gun down."

It doesn't matter what Eugenio says or how calm he remains. Chuck's mind is already made up. Chuck's finger grips the trigger and starts to pull back. The sequential sound of thirty calibre bullets firing disrupts the quietness of the rubbled town. *BANG! BANG!*

Brandishing a gun with a smoking barrel, Eugenio stands on the steps of town hall. Chuck falls to the shale under the light of a full moon as he lies bleeding out, staring into the sky. Michael pats his own body down, frantically checking for a bullet wound.

"Shit! The crazy bastard fuckin' shot me!" Michael looks up to the mayor and shows him a minor cut where the bullet from Chuck's gun grazed his arm. Eugenio stares back, still holding his pistol in the air.

"Michael," Eugenio calmly conveys. Michael remains kneeling with his hands in the air, unresponsive. "Stop being a rich boy for two seconds and get the fuck outta here!"

Michael gets to his feet and slowly backs away. After some odd steps, he turns around and sprints for his life around the corner. Eugenio approaches Chuck. Standing over him, Eugenio locks eyes with Chuck.

"You were like a father to me, Eugenio," Chuck says, lying emotionless.

"You're a dumpster baby, Chuck. I always tried to show you compassion. But you had a chip on your shoulder. And you turned into a monster, a monster that I created," says Eugenio reluctantly.

Chuck sheds a singular tear down his cheek. "You gave me a life … And I'll never forget that." Chuck's head rolls over as it becomes limp.

CHAPTER

The triumphant convoy of garbage trucks returns to the sanitation headquarters heroically, excitedly honking their horns, shooting bullets into the air, and singing a sea shanty the only way you can—very drunkenly.

"The war is over! The war is over!" yells a street child covered in coal stains, following the trucks and struggling to keep up. The garbage workers continue their timeless shanty.

"The war is over! Huzzah!" The dusty child screams, pumping his fist into the air. Smiling as he looks up at the trucks, he stops running and continues to applaud the soldiers. They are welcomed by a parade of family as they enter the barracks. Horace and Patty approach the trucks excitedly to give Chuck a victory hug, looking on as families upon families embrace their loved ones, laughing and dancing. As the crowd slowly clears from the trucks and there is nobody left to unload, they grow restless. Eugenio is the last one to exit. They notice he is with someone and hurry toward them. It is the mayor. Horace and Patty are devastated as Eugenio tells them Chuck did not make it out alive. Eugenio offers his condolences and support.

"If you ever need anything, anything at all, you come to me."

Among the celebratory crowd, Horace and Patty stand dripping tears in each other's arms. "MMNAHHHHHH!" cries out Horace.

Eugenio has business to discuss with the mayor. They sit down in his office, and Eugenio lays out a buffet of cake and cookies for the mayor before imposing his proposition. Graciously willing to devour the dessert offerings he had been waiting for, the mayor is reluctant to accept Eugenio's business terms, but has no choice. Rebuilding the town will cost big money. Although the town has its humble volunteers and some money in their budget, Eugenio is the only person who can front the kind of cash they need to get back to regularity. Eugenio's terms are not unconditional, however.

He crafts himself a golden, get-out-of-jail-free ticket, valid for life. His only ask is that he is able to run his racketeering ring undisturbed — a little bit of illegal gambling, maybe some extortion here and there, but nothing that will get anybody killed. The mayor has no choice but to agree. A handshake closes the dealings, representing a change in power. Eugenio, now some kind of hybrid consigliere, is untouchable in his hometown.

After drinking the night away, it is time to resume their lives. All remaining sanitation workers head towards Gigi's sailboat. Docked in a marina surrounded by expensive and luxurious yachts lay what some would call a ball of floating garbage, a functional eyesore made of recycled barrels and materials. Newfound political prisoner Gigi and her partner Horace hold hands as they stare back into the barren town. They are the last two people to enter the ship. Horace, with one foot on the swaying dock and one foot on the ship, looks back in the distance towards the town. A man is scurrying towards them. It is the mayor. He waves and extends out his arms to the vessel.

"WAIT!" the mayor yells, running like the village idiot. Horace lets go of Gigi's hand and goes to the mayor, who apologizes for the death of Horace's father but believes it should not be in vain. The mayor has plans to rebuild the town. The construction will end with the installation of a statue of Chuck in the town square. The mayor wants to show people that disaster inspires change and that the real disaster would be to keep living like this never happened, stubbornly passing the blame on to the next person until there is no one left to blame. That's who Chuck was, the last person to blame for the town's problems.

"I want you to be the face of a new era, Horace," says the mayor. Gigi comes down from the dock to see what they are talking about. Horace asks Gigi if she wants to stay and help fix the town. In her heart, she wants to stay, but in her mind, she knows they are stronger alone. Love cannot triumph while the world continues to burn.

"Redeem your father, Horace," says Gigi compassionately. They exchange one last kiss, and Gigi walks back over to the dock a refugee to love as Horace watches. The mayor puts his arm around Horace's shoulder.

"Damn, I can't believe you tapped that."

Gigi boards her vessel and sails off, heading to wherever the world needs her next. With a newfound crew of ex-sanitation revolutionaries, she is now something of a political pirate. Gigi and the remaining trash workers drift into the abyss on a giant ball of garbage. Standing at the tip of the bow, Gigi and Horace lock eyes. Whether it is for the last time, they do not know.